The Witching Hour

Riku Fryderyk

The Witching Hour

Nightingale Books

NIGHTINGALE PAPERBACK

A CIP catalogue record for this title is
available from the British Library.
ISBN 9781838751036

Nightingale Books is an imprint of
Pegasus Elliot MacKenzie Publishers Ltd.
www.pegasuspublishers.com

First Published in 2021

Nightingale Books
Sheraton House Castle Park
Cambridge England

Printed & Bound in Great Britain

Dedication

To my little brother, Nico, who always makes me smile.

The red, enormous ball of the sun hid shyly behind the clouds and the ghostly figure of the moon called out the wicked to rise together and show themselves to the world. A cackling voice was heard, calling for the dark to come out from their hiding places.

Magical creatures started to rise up from the underground, concrete pavements became muddy and bounced up and down like boiling potions. Souls from above fluttered down, twisting through the pipes of buildings, checking curiously on their sleeping families.

Abandoned houses grew legs and hands, coming to life. Not a single human being stirred in their beds. All of the city was in a deep, wondrous dream, whilst ugly witches flew on their broomsticks to make sure everyone was asleep.

If anyone did wake up, the smallest spark of magic would make them fall straight back to bed. That was The Witching Hour.

A beautiful sight appeared from behind the mist. One that would make your eyes stare wide open. A flying library.

Glow worms of a green colour lit the way across a shining bridge that led to a grand, golden entrance with stairs made out of marble stone. The stairs were painted in a mosaic of indescribable colours. Giant gargoyles guarded the library, holding two iron spears crossed through the middle of the double doors.

A great-great-great-grandfather clock that sat on the top of the library chimed for The Witching Hour to begin.

In the palace, in the middle of the night, a prince from the royal family was feeling bored. No, even worse, he felt stuck. His family barely ever went out, and to add to that, he wasn't allowed out the grounds of the palace. Not a single time in all eternity. But he wasn't going to stay just like that for his whole life.

He broke out of his royal home and as quiet as a mouse,
tip-toed past the sleeping guards.
He squeezed through the iron gates and ran across the muddy,
rainy pavement down the lanes of the middle-class district.

Unexpectedly,
the prince noticed flying houses,
and pavements moving swiftly like waves.
This peculiar sight amazed him
and made him want to go further and discover more.

Being the first boy to see true magic in this world, the little prince jumped up and down with excitement, and doing so, realised that he could fly in the air as easily as a bird. But that was only the beginning of the power affecting him. Gradually, he started to float like a feather from window to window, getting higher and higher up in the air.

An enormous, beaming smile began to grow on his face, and he whooped with laughter as he twirled in the air, not a care in the world. And in that moment, the witches, the flying houses, dragons and all the other types of mythical creatures that you can imagine, joined him.

He felt better than ever before, being out of the palace, he finally felt free. He also felt wild, like he was able to do anything he wanted and travel the world in search of adventure.

When he got tired and wanted to rest, he sat on a tall, wooden rooftop of a random house and wondered what he could do next. He looked up at the sky, and gazed at the clouds, stars and meteors. Suddenly, an idea popped into his head.

The little boy
called a witch, and whispered something
into her ear.
She listened carefully
and nodded.

And as fast as anything had ever happened,
meteors twirled around
and stars glistened,
both showing
a huge beam of light.

A beautiful rainbow appeared
with sparkling colours,
while puffs of sweet-smelling smoke billowed in the sky.

Witches on broomsticks
flew faster and faster around them,
laughing gleefully while dropping
tiny colourful bombs around them, creating the most wonderful display
anyone had ever seen before.

Lights shone all over London. Children woke up, ran to their windows and rubbed their eyes in disbelief of this spectacular sight. All the children jumped from their windows, not paying any attention to the cold weather, as they wanted to join in the fun. Witches made a magical festive party, with a glamorous glass ball, notes soaring through the air and music playing. There were also some scrumptious raspberry pies that a jolly witch baked for everyone.

Toddlers played with the colourful clouds, whilst older children learnt how to fly on broomsticks with the witches. Everyone had a wonderous time, especially the prince.

***

It turns out that you can get something good out of what may appear to be scary at first. There is nothing to be afraid of, even in the darkest hour.

***

The prince flew swiftly, up and up, and noticed the magnificent building, the flying library. He hadn't read for a while now, so he was ready and hungry for something exciting to read.

The creaky front door opened
with a huge puff of wind from the inside.
He entered the library,
not knowing what was awaiting him…

A colourful cat with sparkling white teeth strolled up to the prince, and passed him a warm, brightly lit lantern. The little boy and the cat walked further into the library, stepping on the dusty creaky floorboards.

The little boy looked around the library, marvelling at it from top to bottom. The prince took out a book from one of the shelves and unexpectedly, an enormous wall rose up, leaving them in a labyrinth of mirrors.

After hours spent on trying to get to the other side of the labyrinth, the prince and the cat reached two sets of doors.

One was big and marked, 'Wonderland' and the other was tiny and marked, 'Quiet Reading Corner'. The cat said that he was going to go and save Alice, his friend. So he went, striding into the green garden that was beyond the door. Slowly and carefully, the prince opened the tiny door and squeezed through it.

A fire crackled in the fireplace, which illuminated the room with a cosy light.
A comfy, wooden rocking chair stood next to it while piles of books nestled in every edge and corner of the room.
The bookshelves were painted in exotic colours and a beautiful, tall, wooden table stood right next to the rocking chair, to make it easier to fish for a new book after finishing one.

The prince sat down on the chair and started reading.
He floated into a different world, a world where anything was possible.
He noticed another door in the room. The prince was sleepy by now, and hoped that the door would lead to a bedroom.

He was right. When he went through the door, indeed there was a bedroom behind it…

The little boy's adventure ends where it all started, in the same bed, in the same room, in the same palace.

THE END

About the Author

Riku Fryderyk, born in London, is a ten-year-old boy who has a passion for writing. He started writing stories at a very early age, with *The Witching Hour* being his first big publication. In the story, Riku wants to help children who are afraid of the dark by making them think differently of what might be there that they cannot see. He shows the powerful side of imagination introducing the reader to the world of magic at its best.